Animal
BEDTIME TALES

Brown Watson
ENGLAND
© 2007 Brown Watson, England
Reprinted 2007, 2010

Jungle Sports Day

Today is Sports Day for the jungle animals and the first event is the three-legged race. All the animals form a line: Giraffe, Rhino and Elephant are strapped together; Lion, Zebra and Crocodile are also tied together; and Tortoise, Sloth and Turtle form the third group. The bigger animals snigger when they see this little trio, they don't think there will be any competition from them!

Hippo raises the starting flag. 'Ready, steady, GO!'

As they whiz past the coconut palms, Elephant's group are just in front. They round a corner and head towards a tangle of jungle vines. 'Duck!' cries Rhino. But it's too late, Giraffe's neck becomes entangled in the vines and they grind to a halt. Lion, Zebra and Crocodile surge ahead but they don't see the huge, sticky spider's web which is stretched across the track.

2

Far behind everyone else, the final little trio plod on. They are very surprised when they overtake Elephant's group, frantically trying to pull Giraffe free. They are even more surprised when they pass Lion's group, all caught up in a giant, sticky web. But they simply can't believe it when they hobble past the finishing post in first place. Turtle, Sloth and Tortoise are the winners and they receive a wonderful trophy. Well done to the slow coaches!

The Forgetful Koala

Kelly Koala is always in trouble because she finds it so hard to remember things.

She forgets to tell Mummy Koala when she goes out to play, she forgets to put her watch on, she forgets her lunch and her homework. Sometimes she even forgets to go to school!

Every morning when she gets out of bed, Kelly knows she is going to forget something important, but she doesn't know what to do about it.

Katie Kangaroo feels very sorry for Kelly and tries to think of a way to help her remember some of the most important things.

She finds a little notepad and pencil in a cupboard at home and takes it round to Kelly's house. Now Kelly can write down everything that she needs to remember. 'What a good idea,' thinks Kelly. But she's so absent minded that she keeps forgetting where she has left the notepad!

Katie thinks this is really funny because she knows an absolutely perfect place for Kelly to keep her notepad and pencil. Like Katie, and lots of other Australian animals, Kelly is a marsupial.

Female marsupials have a little pouch or pocket near their tummies. This is where the mummies keep their babies when they are small and it is the perfect place for Kelly to keep her notepad. She hardly ever forgets anything now!

Fat Cat

Tommy's cat is getting fat. She seems to get rounder everyday! Tommy tells his mum that he's worried Fliss might burst if she keeps on growing. Mummy tells Tommy not to worry because Fliss isn't being greedy. She has lots of babies growing in her tummy, and they could be born at any time. When Tommy gently strokes Fliss's tummy, he can feel the babies moving inside.

One day, when Tommy gets back from school, his mummy calls him into the kitchen. He discovers Fliss surrounded by eight mewing bundles of fur. All the kittens have their eyes closed. When the kittens are old enough to leave their mum, they will all go to good homes, but Tommy pleads to be able to keep one. Mummy agrees and Tommy chooses a little black one with a white mark on her nose. He decides to call her Floss. Isn't Tommy lucky!

Spikey Solutions

Holly Hedgehog wakes up one sunny winter's day and pokes her spiky head out of the crisp pile of leaves she has been sleeping under. Holly has been asleep for two whole months now, although some years she sleeps for even longer. It is unusual for Holly to be awake during the day, but she thinks it might be nice to stretch her legs and go for a stroll!

On her way across the garden, Holly spots Ricky Robin flitting to and fro with scraps of bread and bacon rind in his beak.

He is collecting food for a party at the oak tree at one o'clock, but it is already five minutes to one and Ricky is worried that his friends will arrive before he is ready. He can only carry one scrap of food in his beak on each journey and Holly notices that he is very tired. Then she thinks of a clever way to help.

She curls up into a spiky ball and rolls around the lawn. All the bits of food stick to her prickles. She does look funny!

Holly collects all the food and trots across the grass to the oak tree just as the guests are arriving. Martha Mouse and Scarlet Squirrel have come together, Belinda Bluebird has flown and finally Cyrill Snail slithered across the garden slowly. Ricky Robin is delighted and invites Holly to join them.

Holly has a lovely afternoon with all her friends, but as the sun begins to sink in the sky, it becomes very cold again. Holly suddenly feels very sleepy now, so she says goodbye to everyone and shuffles back across the lawn to her cosy nest of leaves. As the last leaf settles over her head, Holly gives a gentle snore. She is already fast asleep! What a wonderful day she has had.

7

Fergie's Homework

Fergie Frog has some very hard homework to do today. Maths really isn't his favourite subject, he'd much rather be playing with his brothers and sisters. Fergie can count all the way up to twenty, but when he has to add and take away numbers, it becomes much too tricky. Mummy Frog sees him struggling with his homework and thinks of a simpler way to do his sums.

Mummy calls all the family over to the pond. It is a big family and altogether Fergie has nine brothers and six sisters! Mummy is going to use all the children to help Fergie with his sums.

This is the first sum...

$$7 + 5 - 3 =$$

Mummy sends seven of Fergie's brothers over to a lily pad. They splash across the water, climb out and stand in line. Then she sends five of the sisters to join them.

Mummy tells three of the little frogs to jump back in the pond. 'Now Fergie, count how many frogs are left on the lily pad,' she says.

Fergie counts to nine. It's such an easy way to do maths homework! Fergie sends the frogs back and forth across the pond until all his sums are finished. Everyone enjoys themselves and Fergie manages to play with his family and do his homework correctly!

Tomorrow's homework is going to be geography, I wonder if that will be fun too!

Clever Miss Snake

It is Saturday morning and Fenella Flamingo, Gail Gazelle, Jillie Giraffe and Hetty Hippo are going to their ballet lesson. They are very excited because this is the last rehearsal before tonight's big show. They have had to leave Ziggy Zebra behind because she has a bad cold and they are feeling a little worried because Ziggy takes care of all the jobs that need doing off stage.

They each take turns to move the scenery, control the lights, take charge of the curtains and keep the music playing while Miss Snake keeps an eye on the dancing. Everyone is eager to try out new jobs and can't wait for the evening to start. The ballet show is a big success and the audience are very impressed with the teamwork when they know a key member is missing. They give the friends an extra round of applause for doing such a good job. Clever Miss Snake!

The friends want everything to run smoothly as all their families will be seated in the front row. Miss Snake, the ballet teacher, can see how nervous the four friends are and feels sorry for them. She thinks of a way to get all the jobs running smoothly.

Miss Snake tells the class that she needs someone to do some very important jobs as well as dancing. Nobody wants to give up all their dance routines so each dancer has one small job to do, while the others dance.

Olly to the Rescue

Olly Octopus has moved to a new home in the ocean. He is quite a shy octopus and finds it hard to make new friends. Poor Olly is feeling rather lonely.

One day as he is swimming along the ocean floor, he hears a cry for help. Sally Swordfish is trapped under a pile of heavy boulders and Sammy Shark and Daisy Dolphin are trying to push the rocks away to free her. As soon as one rock is pushed aside another slides down in its place.

It is a hopeless task and Olly sees that Sally is really upset. What Sammy and Daisy need is someone to hold back each rock as it is pushed to one side. They need a few extra hands, and guess what? Olly has eight! Sammy and Daisy begin clearing the rocks one by one until Olly is holding on to eight big boulders. Finally Sally can escape. She shoots out of the rocks and gives Olly a big hug. Now he's a hero and everyone wants to be his friend.

Sally Spider

Sally Spider lives in the wood, half way up a sycamore tree, with lots of spider friends.

Each day they make new webs by spinning and weaving threads of silk into wonderful webs. Spiders live in their webs but they are also sticky traps for flies, which is how spiders catch their food.

Because Sally is a very quick weaver, she usually finishes her web by lunchtime and then has nothing else to do for the rest of the day. In summer there are lots of other creatures around to chat to, but in chilly winter everyone comes out of their burrows and nests just long enough to find some food, then they rush back to their warm homes.

Sally thinks that if she could keep her friends warm, they might stay around for a chat. She knows exactly what to do. All afternoon she spins and weaves until she has a pile of long, thin webs. The other spiders are puzzled because these are the strangest webs they've ever seen! 'Whatever is she up to?' they wonder. The next day they find out.

As Ruby Robin flies past, Sally calls out to her. 'Would you like a nice warm scarf, Ruby?'

Ruby is delighted and chats for ages! A little later on, Henry Hare hops by, and Sally asks, 'Would you like a nice warm scarf, Henry?'

Henry is so pleased he stays till teatime. Now everybody wants a scarf and Sally is never bored. She spins and chats all day long!

Alphabet Animals

Wise Old Owl teaches in Bluebell Wood School every morning.

Today, Owl wants his pupils to name one creature for every letter of the alphabet so that they can write a poem. Each of the eight pupils has three letters.

Bunny has ABC, Fox has DEF, Hen has GHI, Kingfisher has JKL, Mouse has MNO, Squirrel has PRS, Vole has TUV, Worm has WYZ and Owl has the two most difficult letters, Q and X.

Everyone makes their list, then Owl helps them with the rhyme.

A is an ALLIGATOR,
a green, scary brute.

B is a BUNNY,
long-eared and cute.

C is for CAT,
with lovely soft fur.

D is a DOG,
who can bark but not purr.

E is for ELEPHANT,
with huge trunk and ears.

F is the FOX,
that Bunny here fears.

G for GIRAFFES,
with long spotty necks.

H is that HEN,
who scratches and pecks.

I for IGUANA,
a scaley reptile.

J for the JACKAL
who's often hostile.

K is KINGFISHER,
who's sitting right here.

L is a LION,
whom I know you all fear.

M is for MOUSE,
so dainty and sweet.

N is for NEWT,
with little webbed feet.

O is for OCTOPUS,
with tentacles, eight!

P is for PENGUIN,
we all think they're great!

Q is a QUEEN BEE,
surrounded by honey.

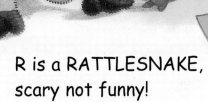

R is a RATTLESNAKE,
scary not funny!

S is for SQUIRREL,
a collector of nuts.

T is the TIGER,
who'll be after your guts!

U is the UNICORN,
made up, not true.

V is for VOLE,
sitting right next to you.

W is WORM,
in that hole by my tree.

X, X-RAY FISH
that live in the sea.

Y is a YAK,
a peculiar sight!

And Z is for ZEBRA,
with stripes, black and white.

No place like home

There are some creatures that love snow, and the colder it gets, the better they like it.

Peggy Penguin lives in the Antarctic, which is down at the bottom of the earth and is a very chilly place to live. Everywhere is white and covered in snow. It is almost always Winter here.

Peggy lives on an iceberg in the sea with a large group of other penguins. Every day they swim and catch fish in the freezing waters.

Every few weeks, large ships, bulging with tourists, stop at Peggy's iceberg to photograph the penguins. These people come from much hotter lands, which Peggy longs to visit because she is tired of being cold. One day Peggy manages to stow away on a ship bound for Italy. She hides amongst boxes and crates until the long journey is finally over and the boat docks.

The sun blazes fiercely over bright flowers, green trees, noisy people and smelly cars.

Peggy is hot, hungry and very homesick. Thoughts of the Antarctic fill her head and she longs for the cool, quiet calm of the iceberg. She hurries back to her hiding place amid the boxes and crates and waits for the ship to sail back north. When she finally gets home, the other penguins want to hear all about her travels. Peggy never dreams about other countries now because she knows, there's no place like home!

The Unhaunted House

Rosie Rat is a timid little creature and all her school friends tease her, so she thinks of a plan to make them think she's brave. At the end of an overgrown lane, close to the wood, stands a tumbledown old house that everyone thinks is haunted. Rosie's school friends are daring each other to spend a night in the old house, but no one is brave enough - except for Rosie!

The other animals can hardly believe that timid little Rosie will go through with it, but they walk with her to the house that night and wave goodbye. The heavy front door creaks open and Rosie disappears inside. As she walks through the house the floorboards squeak and groan. Outside, Rosie's school friends are so scared by the spooky noises that they all run home to bed!

Rosie climbs the rotting staircase and tiptoes into the main bedroom. As she climbs onto the old bed she can hear slow footsteps following up the stairs behind her. Then the bedroom door creaks open. 'Hi, Aunty Ruth and Uncle Ross,' says Rosie. 'Please may I stay for the night?' Rosie's aunt and uncle live here in this quiet old house. Rosie can't wait to see her friends in the morning. She knows they'll never tease her about being timid again!

A Change for Caterpillar

Each morning Snake and Frog follow the same path to the river. One day, as they are passing the big tree where Caterpillar lives, Snake notices something strange hanging from a low branch.

'What do you think that is?' he asks. 'Well it looks like a leaf, but it doesn't match the other leaves,' says Frog. 'Perhaps Caterpillar knows.' But Caterpillar was nowhere to be found!

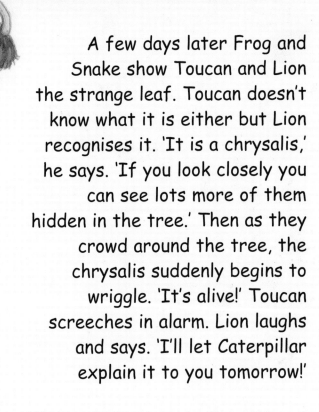

A few days later Frog and Snake show Toucan and Lion the strange leaf. Toucan doesn't know what it is either but Lion recognises it. 'It is a chrysalis,' he says. 'If you look closely you can see lots more of them hidden in the tree.' Then as they crowd around the tree, the chrysalis suddenly begins to wriggle. 'It's alive!' Toucan screeches in alarm. Lion laughs and says. 'I'll let Caterpillar explain it to you tomorrow!'

The next day they gather around the tree. The chrysalis wriggles and shakes until its little sack splits and then out crawls a beautiful butterfly. She flutters around the animals' heads. 'Hi guys, I'm back!' she squeaks. Snake is puzzled. 'I know that voice, but you're not Caterpillar!'

Butterfly smiles. 'For the first part of our lives we are caterpillars, and for the rest we are butterflies. It is still me.' Around them, hundreds of butterflies emerge. Toucan laughs. 'It's all very confusing, but now I can race you to the river!' And they fly off with their friends racing after them.

Untidy Tiger

Timmy Tiger is a very untidy creature. He can never find a thing, and his den is a clutter of rubbish, books and broken toys. One day his friends call round to see if Timmy will play football with them, but he simply cannot find his boots! Three hours later, Timmy finds the boots hidden beneath a pile of clothes, but when he reaches the field, everyone has gone home! If only Timmy's den had not been such a mess! From now on he's going to be a very tidy tiger!

Digging Dennis

Dennis the Dog loves digging holes for his bones. He digs lots of holes all over old Mrs Mottram's garden. Mrs Mottram sighs when she sees her ruined flowerbeds. It will take all day to replant the flowers and she still has the vegetable patch to dig over. Her old bones are aching before she even picks up the spade! Then she has an idea. She gathers up the flowers in a basket, and putting on her hat and coat, she heads off to the florist shop.

The lady at the florist is happy to buy Mrs Mottram's flowers. She can make beautiful flower arrangements to sell in her shop. With the money she receives, Mrs Mottram buys some sausages for tea and a dozen large marrow bones. She gets home and tosses the bones into the vegetable patch. Dennis the Dog is happy to bury the bones, which helpfully digs over the soil. Now it's easy to plant the seeds! It's soon teatime and Mrs Mottram has a big plate of sausage and mash. I think she's earned it, don't you?

Bunny and Honey

Jamie has two cuddly pet rabbits, who live in a hutch at the bottom of his garden. Bunny is a black and white rabbit. He is full of mischief and is always trying to escape. Honey is a large gentle lop-eared rabbit, who just wants to be cuddled. Each morning before school, Jamie cleans out the rabbit hutch and gives them clean water and fresh food.

This morning Jamie hasn't closed the hutch door properly, so Bunny pushes it open with his nose and escapes into the garden. Jamie chases after him but it's too late, Bunny has disappeared. Mummy promises to help look for him after school, so Jamie locks Honey away and hopes Bunny doesn't get too cold outside.

Bunny is very pleased with himself. He nibbles some grass and then goes off to explore the garden.

As the day goes on, Bunny gets hungry and he remembers the juicy carrots and lettuce Jamie brought him that morning. He feels cold and he remembers the fresh warm hay in the hutch. He gets lonely, and worst of all he misses Honey. At four o'clock when Jamie gets home, the first thing he sees is a very unhappy rabbit, huddling next to the hutch. As Jamie opens the door, Bunny rushes in and snuggles next to Honey. Bunny has had his little adventure and he will be quite happy to stay with Honey in future.

Bats and Birds

During Summer the sun doesn't set until quite late in the evening. Jodie is wide-awake in bed even though it is ten o'clock and way past her bedtime. Jodie likes to listen to the birds twittering away before they settle down to sleep. This usually helps her to sleep too. But tonight the birds have quietened down and Jodie still doesn't feel tired.

She opens the curtains and looks out at the moon, in a sky that hasn't yet darkened completely.

She can just make out a few shadowy creatures flitting round and about the house. This puzzles Jodie because all the birds are asleep. What could they be? Mummy pops her head round the door and is surprised to find Jodie is still awake. Jodie says she can't sleep until the birds go to bed. Mummy looks out of the window and chuckles.

She picks a wildlife book from Jodie's bookcase and they read about bats.

When it's dark outside it is easy to mistake bats for birds. Bats are furry and they have leathery wings. They are almost blind but avoid bumping into things by making high-pitched squeaks. The noise bounces off objects and by listening to the echoes, bats can navigate safely. They are nocturnal and they like to hang upside down as they sleep. Jodie is also asleep now. She's upside down too with her feet on the pillow! Mummy tucks her up and kisses her goodnight.

The Jungle Hospital

Leo Lion is in hospital with a broken leg, and he feels very sorry for himself. Nurse Elephant has put his injured leg in plaster and tucked him up in bed. Leo looks around at the other patients. In the next bed is Sally Snake with a sore throat. She is swaddled in thick, woolly scarves to keep her throat warm. Then there is Timmy Tiger who is covered in itchy, red spots and can't stop scratching.

Opposite him is Fenella Flamingo who has eaten something strange and has turned a bit green! No one is talking because they are all too busy feeling sorry for themselves. Suddenly the ward doors are flung open and Philip Frog trundles into the room in a wheelchair. Philip lost both his legs in an accident some time ago, but he is still as full of fun as he's ever been. Nurse Elephant has asked Philip to come in and try to cheer everyone up.

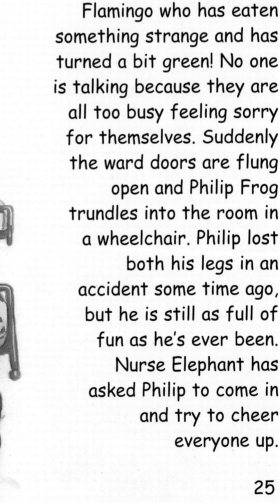

25

Philip spins around the room, talking to everyone and making them smile. Soon the room is buzzing with chatter and laughter. Philip stays for an hour, then leaves, promising to return the next day. Everyone feels so much better after his visit.

Nurse Elephant tells her patients that it is no use feeling sorry for themselves. There's always someone who's worse off than they are.

They nod and smile and chat away for the rest of the day - and they can't wait to see Philip tomorrow!

Wally Warthog's Wish

Wally Warthog lives in the forest. He is covered in bristly, black hair and has a lumpy, bumpy sort of skin and a pair of long, sharp tusks either side of a podgy, little snout. Wally wishes he was handsome and worries that the other forest animals are laughing at him because he is so ugly. He tries to keep away from everyone and that makes him a very lonely warthog.

She is ambling along, pushing her snout through the leaves and looking for something tasty to eat. When she spots him, she smiles at Wally and blushes prettily. Her name is Winnie Warthog and she thinks Wally is the most handsome creature she has ever seen! Wally thinks Winnie is beautiful too. For the first time in their lives, the two warthogs feel happy with the way they look. They decide they were made for each other and live happily ever after.

Wally sees Freddy Fox and wishes he had beautiful red fur. He sees Sally squirrel and wishes he had a fantastic, bushy tail like she does. He sees Milly and Molly Mouse and wishes he had a dainty little nose like they do. Then he sees someone new to the forest, although there is something strangely familiar about her. She has the same shuffling walk as Wally. The same gleaming white tusks. Identical strong, bristly hair and a cute little tail!

A Bad Spell

In the jungle, the animals are playing Blind Man's Bluff, while Little Fairy is fluttering in and out of the trees. What is she looking for? Monkey knows, because he found it earlier that morning. It is a book of very magical spells and, being naughty, he has decided to try one of the spells out on his friends.

The animals blindfold Lion. He has to catch them and guess who each of them is. EASY!

Elephant has flappy ears and a long trunk; Giraffe is tall with a long neck; and Tortoise is so slow!

Then Monkey casts his spell:
'Your shapes I'll change
to something strange.
That flappy ear will disappear,
And what came last
will now be fast!'

Lion catches the first animal. It seems to have small ears, a tiny nose and wrinkly skin. Who can it be?

The next animal has short legs, a short neck and a long tail. Who can this be?

The third animal is impossible to catch because it's moving too fast! Who can this be?

Lion is very confused and takes off his blindfold to see what is happening. All his friends have changed shape. Behind them, high up in the banana tree, he can see Monkey laughing so hard that he nearly loses his balance! Lion opens his mouth to roar at Monkey but all that comes out is a tiny squeak!

Little Fairy sees Monkey clutching her spell book and realises what he's done. She is very cross and grabs the book from Monkey.

'Hear my spell you naughty ape,
I'll turn you yellow
and change your shape.
You must be good
and stop being bad,
Or my spell will last
and you'll be sad!'

In a puff of pink smoke, they all change back, except for Monkey who has suddenly changed into a giant banana! He feels very foolish. The spell will wear off by bedtime, but every time he is naughty he will turn back into a big yellow banana!

I think he will be a very good monkey from now on, don't you?

29

Little Lost Zebra

Little Zebra is lost. He cannot find his mummy and there is no one else around. He begins to worry. There are three paths in front of him, but which is the way back home?

It is very hot so he follows the first track down to the river to have a drink. As he leans forwards a fearsome green head with rows of sharp white teeth explodes out of the water!

Little Zebra is terrified and bolts back to the clearing. Behind him Crocodile climbs out of the water and shakes himself dry.

'Maybe the second path is safer,' thinks Little Zebra. But as he trots along he hears a faint drumming sound. The noise gets closer and closer and louder and louder until the trees begin to shake and the ground trembles. Then a huge grey monster with flapping ears thunders across his path! Little Zebra races back to the clearing once more.

Behind him, Elephant crashes around in the bushes.

'This third path must be the way home,' sobs Little Zebra rushing along.

He stops suddenly as he hears a terrible roar. It is so loud that it makes his ears ring and his legs shake, so he gallops back as fast as he can.

'He's over here!' shouts Lion. 'He's in the clearing.'

Little Zebra is very scared.

He can hear the green sharp-toothed monster splashing up the first path. And the frightening ground-shaking monster is thundering up the second path. And the loud, hairy howling monster is roaring up the third path! HELP!

Then something lifts him high into the air. He squeezes his eyes shut and wishes Mummy was there but it's only Elephant with Crocodile and Lion.

Tired Little Zebra rides on Elephant's back all the way home to his mummy. What an exciting day he has had!

The Sad Little Starfish

Little Starfish lives in the ocean with all the other sea creatures. He is surrounded by crabs, fish, shrimp, sharks and jellyfish, but he'd really like to see someone just like himself. Each night he searches the sea bed, but he can never seem to find another starfish. One night, the waves are much stronger than usual and Little Starfish is washed up onto a beach.

He crawls towards an outcrop of rocks, hoping to find a quiet rock pool to spend the night in. By the time he reaches the rocks he is exhausted, and lies quietly on a stone, gazing up at the night. The sky is awash with twinkling stars, which look a bit like he does! As he is smiling up at the stars, he hears something splashing out of the rock pool. It's another little starfish! She also watches the stars at night and she is lonely too. Now they have met, they will live happily ever after.